'The woods were gradually thinning. I was tormented by strange hallucinations. I gazed at the weird tree trunks, around some of which were coiled thick, flesh-coloured snakes; suddenly I thought I saw, between the trunks, as though through my fingers, the mirror of a half-open wardrobe...'

VLADIMIR NABOKOV

Born 22 April 1899, Saint Petersburg, Russia
Died 2 July 1977, Montreux, Switzerland

'Terra Incognita' [Russian, 1931] first published in English in book form in *A Russian Beauty and Other Stories* (1973). 'Spring in Fialta' [Russian, 1938] first published in English in book form in *Nine Stories* (1947). 'The Doorbell' [Russian, 1930] first published in English in book form in *Details of a Sunset and Other Stories* (1976).

ALSO PUBLISHED BY PENGUIN BOOKS

Laughter in the Dark · *The Real Life of Sebastian Knight* · *Nikolai Gogol* · *Bend Sinister* · *Lolita* · *Pnin* · *Invitation to a Beheading* · *Pale Fire* · *The Gift* · *The Luzhin Defense* · *Despair* · *The Eye* · *Speak, Memory* · *King, Queen, Knave* · *Ada or Ardor* · *Mary* · *Glory* · *Transparent Things* · *Strong Opinions* · *Look at the Harlequins!* · *The Enchanter* · *The Collected Stories* · *The Original of Laura* · *The Collected Poems* · *Letters to Vera*

VLADIMIR NABOKOV

Terra Incognita

PENGUIN BOOKS

PENGUIN CLASSICS

Published by the Penguin Group
Penguin Books Ltd, 80 Strand, London WC2R 0RL, England
Penguin Group (USA) Inc., 375 Hudson Street, New York, New York 10014, USA
Penguin Group (Canada), 90 Eglinton Avenue East, Suite 700, Toronto, Ontario, Canada M4P 2Y3 (a division of Pearson Penguin Canada Inc.)
Penguin Ireland, 25 St Stephen's Green, Dublin 2, Ireland (a division of Penguin Books Ltd)
Penguin Group (Australia), 250 Camberwell Road, Camberwell, Victoria 3124, Australia (a division of Pearson Australia Group Pty Ltd)
Penguin Books India Pvt Ltd, 11 Community Centre, Panchsheel Park, New Delhi – 110 017, India
Penguin Group (NZ), 67 Apollo Drive, Rosedale, North Shore 0632, New Zealand (a division of Pearson New Zealand Ltd)
Penguin Books (South Africa) (Pty) Ltd, 24 Sturdee Avenue, Rosebank, Johannesburg 2196, South Africa
Penguin Books Ltd, Registered Offices: 80 Strand, London WC2R 0RL, England

www.penguin.com

Selected from *Collected Stories*, published in Penguin Classics by arrangement with Weidenfeld & Nicolson, London, and the Estate of Vladimir Nabokov 2010
This edition published in Penguin Classics 2011
4

Typeset by Jouve (UK), Milton Keynes
Printed in England by Clays Ltd, St Ives plc

ISBN: 978-0-141-19616-9

Contents

Terra Incognita

The sound of the waterfall grew more and more muffled, until it finally dissolved altogether, and we moved on through the wildwood of a hitherto unexplored region. We walked, and had been walking, for a long time already – in front, Gregson and I; our eight native porters behind, one after the other; last of all, whining and protesting at every step, came Cook. I knew that Gregson had recruited him on the advice of a local hunter. Cook had insisted that he was ready to do anything to get out of Zonraki, where they pass half the year brewing their *von-gho* and the other half drinking it. It remained unclear, however – or else I was already beginning to forget many things, as we walked on and on – exactly who this Cook was (a runaway sailor, perhaps?).

Gregson strode on beside me, sinewy, lanky, with bare, bony knees. He held a long-handled green butterfly net like a banner. The porters, big, glossy-brown Badonians with thick manes of hair and cobalt arabesques between their eyes, whom we had also engaged in Zonraki, walked with a strong, even step. Behind them straggled Cook, bloated, red-haired, with a drooping underlip, hands in pockets and carrying nothing. I recalled vaguely that at the outset of the expedition he had chattered a lot and made obscure jokes, in a manner he had, a mixture of insolence and servility, reminiscent of a Shakespearean clown; but soon his spirits fell and he grew glum and began to neglect his duties, which included interpreting, since Gregson's understanding of the Badonian dialect was still poor.

There was something languorous and velvety about the heat. A stifling fragrance came from the inflorescences of *Vallieria mirifica*, mother-of-pearl in color and resembling clusters of soap bubbles, that arched across the narrow, dry streambed along which we proceeded. The branches of porphyroferous trees intertwined with those of the black-leafed limia to form a tunnel, penetrated here and there by a ray of hazy light. Above, in the thick mass of vegetation, among brilliant pendulous racemes and strange dark tangles of some kind, hoary monkeys snapped and chattered, while a comet-like bird flashed like Bengal light, crying out in its small, shrill voice. I kept telling myself that my head was heavy from the long march, the heat, the medley of colors, and the forest din, but secretly I knew that I was ill. I surmised it to be the local fever. I had resolved, however, to conceal my condition from Gregson, and had assumed a cheerful, even merry air, when disaster struck.

'It's my fault,' said Gregson. 'I should never have got involved with him.'

We were now alone. Cook and all eight of the natives, with tent, folding boat, supplies, and collections, had deserted us and vanished noiselessly while we busied ourselves in the thick bush, chasing fascinating insects. I think we tried to catch up with the fugitives – I do not recall clearly, but, in any case, we failed. We had to decide whether to return to Zonraki or continue our projected itinerary, across as yet unknown country, toward the Gurano Hills. The unknown won out. We moved on. I was already shivering all over and deafened by quinine, but still went on collecting nameless plants, while Gregson, though fully realizing the danger of our situation, continued catching butterflies and diptera as avidly as ever.

We had scarcely walked half a mile when suddenly Cook overtook us. His shirt was torn – apparently by himself, deliberately – and he was panting and gasping. Without a word Gregson drew his revolver and prepared to shoot the scoundrel, but he threw himself at Gregson's feet and, shielding his head with both arms, began to swear that the natives had led him away by force and had wanted to eat him (which was a lie, for the Badonians are not cannibals). I suspect that he had easily incited them, stupid and timorous as they were, to abandon the dubious journey, but had not taken into account that he could not keep up with their powerful stride and, having fallen hopelessly behind, had returned to us. Because of him invaluable collections were lost. He had to die. But Gregson put away the revolver and we moved on, with Cook wheezing and stumbling behind.

The woods were gradually thinning. I was tormented by strange hallucinations. I gazed at the weird tree trunks, around some of which were coiled thick, flesh-colored snakes; suddenly I thought I saw, between the trunks, as though through my fingers, the mirror of a half-open wardrobe with dim reflections, but then I took hold of myself, looked more carefully, and found that it was only the deceptive glimmer of an acreana bush (a curly plant with large berries resembling plump prunes). After a while the trees parted altogether and the sky rose before us like a solid wall of blue. We were at the top of a steep incline. Below shimmered and steamed an enormous marsh, and, far beyond, one distinguished the tremulous silhouette of a mauve-colored range of hills.

'I swear to God we must turn back,' said Cook in a sobbing voice. 'I swear to God we'll perish in these swamps – I've got seven daughters and a dog at home. Let's turn back – we know the way . . .'

He wrung his hands, and the sweat rolled from his fat, red-browed face. 'Home, home,' he kept repeating. 'You've caught enough bugs. Let's go home!'

Gregson and I began to descend the stony slope. At first Cook remained standing above, a small white figure against the monstrously green background of forest; but suddenly he threw up his hands, uttered a cry, and started to slither down after us.

The slope narrowed, forming a rocky crest that reached out like a long promontory into the marshes; they sparkled through the steamy haze. The noonday sky, now freed of its leafy veils, hung oppressively over us with its blinding darkness – yes, its blinding darkness, for there is no other way to describe it. I tried not to look up; but in this sky, at the very verge of my field of vision, there floated, always keeping up with me, whitish phantoms of plaster, stucco curlicues and rosettes, like those used to adorn European ceilings; however, I had only to look directly at them and they would vanish, and again the tropical sky would boom, as it were, with even, dense blueness. We were still walking along the rocky promontory, but it kept tapering and betraying us. Around it grew golden marsh reeds, like a million bared swords gleaming in the sun. Here and there flashed elongated pools, and over them hung dark swarms of midges. A large swamp flower, presumably an orchid, stretched toward me its drooping, downy lip, which seemed smeared with egg yolk. Gregson swung his net – and sank to his hips in the brocaded ooze as a gigantic swallowtail, with a flap of its satin wing, sailed away from him over the reeds, toward the shimmer of pale emanations where the indistinct folds of a window curtain seemed to hang. *I must not*, I said to myself, *I must not* . . . I shifted my gaze and walked on beside Gregson, now over rock, now across hissing and lip-smacking soil. I felt chills, in spite of the greenhouse heat. I foresaw that in a moment I would collapse altogether, that the contours and convexities of delirium, showing through the sky and through the golden reeds, would gain complete control of my consciousness. At times Gregson and Cook seemed to grow transparent, and I thought I saw, through them, wallpaper with an endlessly repeated design of reeds. I took hold of myself, strained to keep my eyes open, and moved on. Cook by now was crawling on all fours, yelling, and snatching at Gregson's legs, but the latter would shake him off and keep walking. I looked at Gregson, at his stubborn profile, and felt, to my horror, that I was forgetting who Gregson was, and why I was with him.

Meanwhile we kept sinking into the ooze more and more frequently, deeper and deeper; the insatiable mire would suck at us; and, wriggling, we would slip free. Cook kept falling down and crawling, covered with insect bites, all swollen and soaked, and, dear God, how he would squeal when disgusting bevies of minute, bright-green hydrotic snakes, attracted by our sweat, would take off in pursuit of us, tensing and uncoiling to sail two yards and then another two. I, however, was much more frightened by something else: now and then, on my left (always, for some reason, on my left), listing among the repetitious reeds, what seemed a large armchair but was actually a strange, cumbersome gray amphibian, whose name Gregson refused to tell me, would rise out of the swamp.

'A break,' said Gregson abruptly, 'let's take a break.'

By a stroke of luck we managed to scramble on to an islet of rock, surrounded by the swamp vegetation. Gregson took off his knapsack and issued us some native patties, smelling of ipecacuanha, and a dozen acreana fruit. How thirsty I was, and how little help was the scanty, astringent juice of the acreana . . .

'Look, how odd,' Gregson said to me, not in English,

but in some other language, so that Cook would not understand. 'We must get through to the hills, but look, how odd – could the hills have been a mirage? – they are no longer visible.'

I raised myself up from my pillow and leaned my elbow on the resilient surface of the rock . . . Yes, it was true that the hills were no longer visible; there was only the quivering vapor hanging over the marsh. Once again everything around me assumed an ambiguous transparency. I leaned back and said softly to Gregson, 'You probably can't see, but something keeps trying to come through.'

'What are you talking about?' asked Gregson.

I realized that what I was saying was nonsense and stopped. My head was spinning and there was a humming in my ears; Gregson, down on one knee, rummaged through his knapsack, but found no medicine there, and my supply was exhausted. Cook sat in silence, morosely picking at a rock. Through a rent in his shirtsleeve there showed a strange tattoo on his arm: a crystal tumbler with a teaspoon, very well executed.

'Vallière is sick – haven't you got some tablets?' Gregson said to him. I did not hear the exact words, but I could guess the general sense of their talk, which would grow absurd and somehow spherical when I tried to listen more closely.

Cook turned slowly and the glassy tattoo slid off his skin to one side, remaining suspended in midair; then it floated off, floated off, and I pursued it with my frightened gaze, but, as I turned away, it lost itself in the vapor of the swamp, with a last faint gleam.

'Serves you right,' muttered Cook. 'It's just too bad. The same will happen to you and me. Just too bad . . .'

In the course of the last few minutes – that is, ever since we had stopped to rest on the rocky islet – he seemed to have grown larger, had swelled, and there was now something mocking and dangerous about him. Gregson took off his sun helmet and, pulling out a dirty handkerchief, wiped his forehead, which was orange over the brows, and white above that. Then he put on his helmet again, leaned over to me, and said, 'Pull yourself together, please' (or words to that effect). 'We shall try to move on. The vapor is hiding the hills, but they are there. I am certain we have covered about half the swamp.' (This is all very approximate.)

'Murderer,' said Cook under his breath. The tattoo was now again on his forearm; not the entire glass, though, but one side of it – there was not quite enough room for the remainder, which quivered in space, casting reflections. 'Murderer,' Cook repeated with satisfaction, raising his inflamed eyes. 'I told you we would get stuck here. Black dogs eat too much carrion. Mi, re, fa, sol.'

'He's a clown,' I softly informed Gregson, 'a Shakespearean clown.'

'Clow, clow, clow,' Gregson answered, 'clow, clow – clo, clo, clo . . . Do you hear?' he went on, shouting in my ear. 'You must get up. We have to move on.'

The rock was as white and as soft as a bed. I raised myself a little, but promptly fell back on the pillow.

'We shall have to carry him,' said Gregson's faraway voice. 'Give me a hand.'

'Fiddlesticks,' replied Cook (or so it sounded to me). 'I suggest we enjoy some fresh meat before he dries up. Fa, sol, mi, re.'

'He's sick, he's sick too,' I cried to Gregson. 'You're here with two lunatics. Go ahead alone. You'll make it . . . Go.'

'Fat chance we'll let him go,' said Cook.

Meanwhile delirious visions, taking advantage of the general confusion, were quietly and firmly finding their places. The lines of a dim ceiling stretched and crossed in the sky. A large armchair rose, as if supported from below, out of the swamp. Glossy birds flew through the haze of the marsh and, as they settled, one turned into the wooden knob of a bedpost, another into a decanter. Gathering all my willpower, I focused my gaze and drove off this dangerous trash. Above the reeds flew real birds with long flame-colored tails. The air buzzed with insects. Gregson was waving away a varicolored fly, and at the same time trying to determine its species. Finally he could contain himself no longer and caught it in his net. His motions underwent curious changes, as if someone kept reshuffling them. I saw him in different poses simultaneously; he was divesting himself of himself, as if he were made of many glass Gregsons whose outlines did not coincide. Then he condensed again, and stood up firmly. He was shaking Cook by the shoulder.

'You are going to help me carry him,' Gregson was saying distinctly. 'If you were not a traitor, we would not be in this mess.'

Cook remained silent, but slowly flushed purple.

'See here, Cook, you'll regret this,' said Gregson. 'I'm telling you for the last time –'

At this point occurred what had been ripening for a long time. Cook drove his head like a bull into Gregson's stomach. They both fell; Gregson had time to get his revolver out, but Cook managed to knock it out of his hand. Then they clutched each other and started rolling in their embrace, panting deafeningly. I looked at them, helpless. Cook's broad back would grow tense and the vertebrae would show through his shirt; but suddenly, instead of his back, a leg, also his, would appear, covered with coppery hairs, and with a blue vein running up the skin, and Gregson was rolling on top of him. Gregson's helmet flew off and wobbled away, like half of an enormous cardboard egg. From somewhere in the labyrinth of their bodies Cook's fingers wriggled out, clenching a rusty but sharp knife; the knife entered Gregson's back as if it were clay, but Gregson only gave a grunt, and they both rolled over several times; when I next saw my friend's back the handle and top half of the blade protruded, while his hands had locked around Cook's thick neck, which crunched as he squeezed, and Cook's legs were twitching. They made one last full revolution, and now only a quarter of the blade was visible – no, a fifth – no, now not even that much showed: it had entered completely. Gregson grew still after having piled on top of Cook, who had also become motionless.

I watched, and it seemed to me (fogged as my senses were by fever) that this was all a harmless game, that in a moment they would get up and, when they had caught their breath, would peacefully carry me off across the swamp toward the cool blue hills, to some shady place with babbling water. But suddenly, at this last stage of my mortal illness – for I knew that in a few minutes I would die – in these final minutes everything grew completely lucid: I realized that all that was taking place around me was not the trick of an inflamed imagination, not the veil of delirium, through which unwelcome glimpses of my supposedly real existence in a distant European city (the wallpaper, the armchair, the glass of lemonade) were trying to show. I realized that the obtrusive room was fictitious, since everything beyond death is, at best, fictitious: an imitation of life hastily knocked together, the furnished rooms of nonexistence. I realized that reality was here, here beneath that wonderful, frightening tropical sky, among those gleaming swordlike reeds, in that vapor hanging over them, and in the thick-lipped flowers clinging to the flat islet, where, beside me, lay two clinched corpses. And, having realized this, I found within me the strength to crawl over to them and pull the knife from the back of Gregson, my leader, my dear friend. He was dead, quite dead, and all the little bottles in his pockets were broken and crushed. Cook, too, was dead, and his ink-black tongue protruded from his mouth. I pried open Gregson's fingers and turned his body over. His lips were half-open and bloody; his face, which already seemed hardened, appeared badly shaven; the bluish whites of his eyes showed between the lids. For the last time I saw all this distinctly, consciously, with the seal of authenticity on everything – their skinned knees, the bright flies circling over them, the females of those flies already seeking a spot for oviposition. Fumbling with my enfeebled hands,

I took a thick notebook out of my shirt pocket, but here I was overcome by weakness; I sat down and my head drooped. And yet I conquered this impatient fog of death and looked around. Blue air, heat, solitude . . . And how sorry I felt for Gregson, who would never return home – I even remembered his wife and the old cook, and his parrots, and many other things. Then I thought about our discoveries, our precious finds, the rare, still undescribed plants and animals that now would never be named by us. I was alone. Hazier flashed the reeds, dimmer flamed the sky. My eyes followed an exquisite beetle that was crawling across a stone, but I had no strength left to catch it. Everything around me was fading, leaving bare the scenery of death – a few pieces of realistic furniture and four walls. My last motion was to open the book, which was damp with my sweat, for I absolutely had to make a note of something; but, alas, it slipped out of my hand. I groped all along the blanket, but it was no longer there.

Spring in Fialta

Spring in Fialta is cloudy and dull. Everything is damp: the piebald trunks of the plane trees, the juniper shrubs, the railings, the gravel. Far away, in a watery vista between the jagged edges of pale bluish houses, which have tottered up from their knees to climb the slope (a cypress indicating the way), the blurred Mount St George is more than ever remote from its likeness on the picture postcards which since 1910, say (those straw hats, those youthful cabmen), have been courting the tourist from the sorry-go-round of their prop, among amethyst-toothed lumps of rock and the mantelpiece dreams of seashells. The air is windless and warm, with a faint tang of burning. The sea, its salt drowned in a solution of rain, is less glaucous than gray with waves too sluggish to break into foam.

It was on such a day in the early thirties that I found myself, all my senses wide open, on one of Fialta's steep little streets, taking in everything at once, that marine rococo on the stand, and the coral crucifixes in a shop window, and the dejected poster of a visiting circus, one corner of its drenched paper detached from the wall, and a yellow bit of unripe orange peel on the old, slate-blue sidewalk, which retained here and there a fading memory of ancient mosaic design. I am fond of Fialta; I am fond of it because I feel in the hollow of those violaceous syllables the sweet dark dampness of the most rumpled of small flowers, and because the altolike name of a lovely Crimean town is echoed by its viola; and also because there is something in the very somnolence of its humid Lent that especially anoints one's soul. So I was happy to be there again, to trudge uphill in inverse direction to the rivulet of the gutter, hatless, my head wet, my skin already suffused with warmth although I wore only a light mackintosh over my shirt.

I had come on the Capparabella express, which, with that reckless gusto peculiar to trains in mountainous country, had done its thundering best to collect throughout the night as many tunnels as possible. A day or two, just as long as a breathing spell in the midst of a business trip would allow me, was all I expected to stay. I had left my wife and children at home, and that was an island of happiness always present in the dear north of my being, always floating beside me, and even through me, I dare say, but yet keeping on the outside of me most of the time.

A pantless infant of the male sex, with a taut mud-gray little belly, jerkily stepped down from a doorstep and waddled off, bowlegged, trying to carry three oranges at once, but continuously dropping the variable third, until he fell himself, and then a girl of twelve or so, with a string of heavy beads around her dusky neck and wearing a skirt as long as that of a Gypsy, promptly took away the whole lot with her more nimble and more numerous hands. Nearby, on the wet terrace of a café, a waiter was wiping the slabs of tables; a melancholy brigand hawking local lollipops, elaborate-looking things with a lunar gloss, had placed a hopelessly full basket on the cracked balustrade, over which the two were conversing. Either the drizzle had stopped or Fialta had got so used to it that she herself did not know whether she was breathing moist air or warm rain. Thumb-filling his pipe from a rubber pouch as he walked, a plus-foured Englishman of the solid exportable sort came from under an arch and entered a pharmacy, where large pale sponges in a blue vase were dying a thirsty death behind their glass. What luscious elation I felt rippling through my veins, how gratefully my whole being responded to the flutters and effluvia of that gray day saturated with a vernal essence which itself it seemed slow in perceiving! My nerves were unusually receptive after a sleepless night; I assimilated everything: the whistling of a thrush in the almond trees beyond the chapel, the peace of the crumbling houses, the pulse of the distant sea, panting in the mist, all this together with the jealous green of bottle glass bristling along the top of a wall and the fast colors of a circus advertisement featuring a feathered Indian on a rearing horse in the act of lassoing a boldly endemic zebra, while some thoroughly fooled elephants sat brooding upon their star-spangled thrones.

Presently the same Englishman overtook me. As I absorbed him along with the rest, I happened to notice the sudden side-roll of his big blue eye straining at its crimson canthus, and the way he rapidly moistened his lips – because of the dryness of those sponges, I thought; but then I followed the direction of his glance, and saw Nina.

Every time I had met her during the fifteen years of our – well, I fail to find the precise term for our kind of relationship – she had not seemed to recognize me at once; and this time too she remained quite still for a moment, on the opposite sidewalk, half turning toward me in sympathetic incertitude mixed with curiosity, only her yellow scarf already on the move like those dogs that recognize you before their owners do – and then she uttered a cry, her hands up, all her ten fingers dancing, and in the middle of the street, with merely the frank impulsiveness of an old friendship (just as she would rapidly make the sign of the cross over me every time we parted), she kissed me thrice with more mouth than meaning, and then walked beside me, hanging on to me, adjusting her stride to mine, hampered by her narrow brown skirt perfunctorily slit down the side.

'Oh, yes, Ferdie is here too,' she replied and immediately in her turn inquired nicely after Elena.

'Must be loafing somewhere around with Segur,' she went on in reference to her husband. 'And I have some shopping to do; we leave after lunch. Wait a moment, where are you leading me, Victor dear?'

Back into the past, back into the past, as I did every time I met her, repeating the whole accumulation of the plot from the very beginning up to the last increment – thus in Russian fairy tales the already told is bunched up again at every new turn of the story. This time we had met in warm and misty Fialta, and I could not have celebrated the occasion with greater art, could not have adorned with brighter vignettes the list of fate's former services, even if I had known that this was to be the last one; the last one, I maintain, for I cannot imagine any heavenly firm of brokers that might consent to arrange me a meeting with her beyond the grave.

My introductory scene with Nina had been laid in Russia quite a long time ago, around 1917 I should say, judging by certain left-wing theater rumblings backstage. It was at some birthday party at my aunt's on her country estate, near Luga, in the deepest folds of winter (how well I remember the first sign of nearing the place: a red barn in a white wilderness). I had just graduated from the Imperial Lyceum; Nina was already engaged: although she was of my age and of that of the century, she looked twenty at least, and this in spite or perhaps because of her neat slender build, whereas at thirty-two that very slightness of hers made her look younger. Her fiancé was a guardsman on leave from the front, a handsome heavy fellow, incredibly well bred and stolid, who weighed every word on the scales of the most exact common sense and spoke in a velvety baritone, which grew even smoother when he addressed her; his decency and devotion probably got on her nerves; and he is now a successful if somewhat lonesome engineer in a most distant tropical country.

Windows light up and stretch their luminous lengths upon the dark billowy snow, making room for the reflection of the fan-shaped light above the front door between them. Each of the two side pillars is fluffily fringed with white, which rather spoils the lines of what might have been a perfect ex libris for the book of our two lives. I cannot recall why we had all wandered out of the sonorous hall into the still darkness, peopled only with firs, snow-swollen to twice their size; did the watchmen invite us to look at a sullen red glow in the sky, portent of nearing arson? Possibly. Did we go to admire an equestrian statue of ice sculptured near the pond by the Swiss tutor of my cousins? Quite as likely. My memory revives only on the way back to the brightly symmetrical mansion toward which we tramped in single file along a narrow farrow between snowbanks, with that crunch-crunch-crunch which is the only comment that a taciturn winter night makes upon humans. I walked last; three singing steps ahead of me walked a small bent shape; the firs gravely showed their burdened paws. I slipped and dropped the dead flashlight someone had forced upon me; it was devilishly hard to retrieve; and instantly attracted by my curses, with an eager, low laugh in anticipation of fun, Nina dimly veered toward me. I call her Nina, but I could hardly have known her name yet, hardly could we have had time, she and I, for any preliminary; 'Who's that?' she asked with interest – and I was already kissing her neck, smooth and quite fiery hot from the long fox fur of her coat collar, which kept getting into my way until she clasped my shoulder, and with the candor so peculiar to her gently fitted her generous, dutiful lips to mine. But suddenly parting us by its explosion of gaiety, the theme of a snowball fight started in the dark, and someone, fleeing, falling, crunching, laughing, and panting, climbed a drift, tried to run, and uttered a horrible groan: deep snow had performed the amputation of an arctic. And soon after, we all dispersed to our respective homes, without my having talked with Nina, nor made any plans about the future, about those fifteen itinerant years that had already set out toward the dim horizon, loaded with the parts of our unassembled meetings; and as I watched her in the maze of gestures and shadows of gestures of which the rest of that evening consisted (probably parlor games – with Nina persistently in the other camp), I was astonished, I remember, not so much by her inattention to me after that warmth in the snow as by the innocent naturalness of that inattention, for I did not yet know that had I said a word it would have changed at once into a wonderful sunburst of kindness, a cheerful, compassionate attitude with all possible cooperation, as if woman's love were springwater containing salubrious salts which at the least notice she ever so willingly gave anyone to drink.

'Let me see, where did we last meet,' I began (addressing the Fialta version of Nina) in order to bring to her small face with prominent cheekbones and dark-red lips a certain expression I knew, and sure enough, the shake of her head and the puckered brow seemed less to imply forgetfulness than to deplore the flatness of an old joke; or to be more exact, it was as if all those cities where fate had fixed our various rendezvous without ever attending them personally, all those platforms and stairs and three-walled rooms and dark back alleys, were trite settings remaining after some other lives all brought to a close long before and were so little related to the acting out of our own aimless destiny that it was almost bad taste to mention them.

I accompanied her into a shop under the arcades; there, in the twilight beyond a beaded curtain, she fingered some red leather purses stuffed with tissue paper, peering at the price tags, as if wishing to learn their museum names. She wanted, she said, exactly that shape but in fawn, and when after ten minutes of frantic rustling the old Dalmatian found such a freak by a miracle that has puzzled me ever since, Nina, who was about to pick some money out of my hand, changed her mind and went through the streaming beads without having bought anything.

Outside it was just as milky dull as before; the same smell of burning, stirring my Tartar memories, drifted from the bare windows of the pale houses; a small swarm of gnats was busy darning the air above a mimosa, which bloomed listlessly, her sleeves trailing to the very ground; two workmen in broad-brimmed hats were lunching on cheese and garlic, their backs against a circus billboard, which depicted a red hussar and an orange tiger of sorts; curious – in his effort to make the beast as ferocious as possible, the artist had gone so far that he had come back from the other side, for the tiger's face looked positively human.

'*Au fond*, I wanted a comb,' said Nina with belated regret.

How familiar to me were her hesitations, second thoughts, third thoughts mirroring first ones, ephemeral worries between trains. She had always either just arrived or was about to leave, and of this I find it hard to think without feeling humiliated by the variety of intricate routes one feverishly follows in order to keep that final appointment which the most confirmed dawdler knows to be unavoidable. Had I to submit before judges of our earthly existence a specimen of her average pose, I would have perhaps placed her leaning upon a counter at Cook's, left calf crossing right shin, left toe tapping floor, sharp elbows and coin-spilling bag on the counter, while the employee, pencil in hand, pondered with her over the plan of an eternal sleeping car.

After the exodus from Russia, I saw her – and that was the second time – in Berlin at the house of some friends. I was about to get married; she had just broken with her fiancé. As I entered that room I caught sight of her at once and, having glanced at the other guests, I instinctively determined which of the men knew more about her than I. She was sitting in the corner of a couch, her feet pulled up, her small comfortable body folded in the form of a Z; an ashtray stood aslant on the couch near one of her heels; and, having squinted at me and listened to my name, she removed her stalklike cigarette holder from her lips and proceeded to utter slowly and joyfully, 'Well, of all people—' and at once it became clear to everyone, beginning with her, that we had long been on intimate terms: unquestionably, she had forgotten all about the actual kiss, but somehow because of that trivial occurrence she found herself recollecting a vague sketch of warm, pleasant friendship, which in reality had never existed between us. Thus the whole cast of our relationship was fraudulently based upon an imaginary amity – which had nothing to do with her random good will. Our meeting proved quite insignificant in regard to the words we said, but already no barriers divided us; and when that night I happened to be seated beside her at supper, I shamelessly tested the extent of her secret patience.

Then she vanished again; and a year later my wife and I were seeing my brother off to Posen, and when the train had gone, and we were moving toward the exit along the other side of the platform, suddenly near a car of the Paris express I saw Nina, her face buried in the bouquet she held, in the midst of a group of people whom she had befriended without my knowledge and who stood in a circle gaping at her as idlers gape at a street row, a lost child, or the victim of an accident. Brightly she signaled to me with her flowers; I introduced her to Elena, and in that life-quickening atmosphere of a big railway station where everything is something trembling on the brink of something else, thus to be clutched and cherished, the exchange of a few words was enough to enable two totally dissimilar women to start calling each other by their pet names the very next time they met. That day, in the blue shade of the Paris car, Ferdinand was first mentioned: I learned with a ridiculous pang that she was about to marry him. Doors were beginning to slam; she quickly but piously kissed her friends, climbed into the vestibule, disappeared; and then I saw her through the glass settling herself in her compartment, having suddenly forgotten about us or passed into another world, and we all, our hands in our pockets, seemed to be spying upon an utterly unsuspecting life moving in that aquarium dimness, until she grew aware of us and drummed on the windowpane, then raised her eyes, fumbling at the frame as if hanging a picture, but nothing happened; some fellow passenger helped her, and she leaned out, audible and real, beaming with pleasure; one of us, keeping up with the stealthily gliding car, handed her a magazine and a Tauchnitz (she read English only when traveling); all was slipping away with beautiful smoothness, and I held a platform ticket crumpled beyond recognition, while a song of the last century (connected, it has been rumored, with some Parisian drama of love) kept ringing and ringing in my head, having emerged, God knows why, from the music box of memory, a sobbing ballad which often used to be sung by an old maiden aunt of mine, with a face as yellow as Russian church wax, but whom nature had given such a powerful, ecstatically full voice that it seemed to swallow her up in the glory of a fiery cloud as soon as she would begin:

On dit que tu te maries,
tu sais que j'en vais mourir

and that melody, the pain, the offense, the link between hymen and death evoked by the rhythm, and the voice itself of the dead singer, which accompanied the recollection as the sole owner of the song, gave me no rest for several hours after Nina's departure and even later arose at increasing intervals like the last flat little waves sent to the beach by a passing ship, lapping ever more infrequently and dreamily, or like the bronze agony of a vibrating belfry after the bell ringer has already reseated himself in the cheerful circle of his family. And another year or two later, I was in Paris on business; and one morning on the landing of a hotel, where I had been looking up a film actor fellow, there she was again, clad in a gray tailored suit, waiting for the elevator to take her down, a key dangling from her fingers. 'Ferdinand has gone fencing,' she said conversationally; her eyes rested on the lower part of my face as if she were lip reading, and after a moment of reflection (her amatory comprehension was matchless), she turned and rapidly swaying on slender ankles led me along the sea-blue carpeted passage. A chair at the door of her room supported a tray with the remains of breakfast – a honey-stained knife, crumbs on the gray porcelain; but the room had already been done, and because of our sudden draft a wave of muslin embroidered with white dahlias got sucked in, with a shudder and knock, between the responsive halves of the French window, and only when the door had been locked did they let go that curtain with something like a blissful sigh; and a little later I stepped out on the diminutive cast-iron balcony beyond to inhale a combined smell of dry maple leaves and gasoline – the dregs of the hazy blue morning street; and as I did not yet realize the presence of that growing morbid pathos which was to embitter so my subsequent meetings with Nina, I was probably quite as collected and carefree as she was, when from the hotel I accompanied her to some office or other to trace a suitcase she had lost, and thence to the café where her husband was holding session with his court of the moment.

I will not mention the name (and what bits of it I happen to give here appear in decorous disguise) of that man, that Franco-Hungarian writer . . . I would rather not dwell upon him at all, but I cannot help it – he is surging up from under my pen. Today one does not hear much about him; and this is good, for it proves that I was right in resisting his evil spell, right in experiencing a creepy chill down my spine whenever this or that new book of his touched my hand. The fame of his likes circulates briskly but soon grows heavy and stale; and as for history it will limit his life story to the dash between two dates. Lean and arrogant; with some poisonous pun ever ready to fork out and quiver at you, and with a strange look of expectancy in his dull brown veiled eyes, this false wag had, I daresay, an irresistible effect on small rodents. Having mastered the art of verbal invention to perfection, he particularly prided himself on being a weaver of words, a title he valued higher than that of a writer; personally, I never could understand what was the good of thinking up books, of penning things that had not really happened in some way or other; and I remember once saying to him as I braved the mockery of his encouraging nods that, were I a writer, I should allow only my heart to have imagination, and for the rest rely upon memory, that long-drawn sunset shadow of one's personal truth.

I had known his books before I knew him; a faint disgust was already replacing the aesthetic pleasure which I had suffered his first novel to give me. At the beginning of his career, it had been possible perhaps to distinguish some human landscape, some old garden, some dream-familiar disposition of trees through the stained glass of his prodigious prose . . . but with every new book the tints grew still more dense, the gules and purpure still more ominous; and today one can no longer see anything at all through that blazoned, ghastly rich glass, and it seems that were one to break it, nothing but a perfectly black void would face one's shivering soul. But how dangerous he was in his prime, what venom he squirted, with what whips he lashed when provoked! The tornado of his passing satire left a barren waste where felled oaks lay in a row, and the dust still twisted, and the unfortunate author of some adverse review, howling with pain, spun like a top in the dust.

At the time we met, his *Passage à niveau* was being acclaimed in Paris; he was, as they say, 'surrounded,' and Nina (whose adaptability was an amazing substitute for the culture she lacked) had already assumed if not the part of a muse at least that of a soul mate and subtle adviser, following Ferdinand's creative convolutions and loyally sharing his artistic tastes; for although it is wildly improbable that she had ever waded through a single volume of his, she had a magic knack of gleaning all the best passages from the shop talk of literary friends.

An orchestra of women was playing when we entered the café; first I noted the ostrich thigh of a harp reflected in one of the mirror-faced pillars, and then I saw the composite table (small ones drawn together to form a long one) at which, with his back to the plush wall, Ferdinand was presiding; and for a moment his whole attitude, the position of his parted hands, and the faces of his table companions all turned toward him reminded me in a grotesque, nightmarish way of something I did not quite grasp, but when I did so in retrospect, the suggested comparison struck me as hardly less sacrilegious than the nature of his art itself. He wore a white turtleneck sweater under a tweed coat;

his glossy hair was combed back from the temples, and above it cigarette smoke hung like a halo; his bony, pharaohlike face was motionless: the eyes alone roved this way and that, full of dim satisfaction. Having forsaken the two or three obvious haunts where naive amateurs of Montparnassian life would have expected to find him, he had started patronizing this perfectly bourgeois establishment because of his peculiar sense of humor, which made him derive ghoulish fun from the pitiful *spécialité de la maison* – this orchestra composed of half a dozen weary-looking, self-conscious ladies interlacing mild harmonies on a crammed platform and not knowing, as he put it, what to do with their motherly bosoms, quite superfluous in the world of music. After each number he would be convulsed by a fit of epileptic applause, which the ladies had stopped acknowledging and which was already arousing, I thought, certain doubts in the minds of the proprietor of the café and its fundamental customers, but which seemed highly diverting to Ferdinand's friends. Among these I recall: an artist with an impeccably bald though slightly chipped head, which under various pretexts he constantly painted into his eye-and-guitar canvases; a poet, whose special gag was the ability to represent, if you asked him, Adam's Fall by means of five matches; a humble businessman who financed surrealist ventures (and paid for the aperitifs) if permitted to print in a corner eulogistic allusions to the actress he kept; a pianist, presentable insofar as the face was concerned, but with a dreadful expression of the fingers; a jaunty but linguistically impotent Soviet writer fresh from Moscow, with an old pipe and a new wristwatch, who was completely and ridiculously unaware of the sort of company he was in; there were several other gentlemen present who have become confused in my memory, and doubtless two or three of the lot had been intimate with Nina. She was the only woman at the table; there she stooped, eagerly sucking at a straw, the level of her lemonade sinking with a kind of childish celerity, and only when the last drop had gurgled and squeaked, and she had pushed away the straw with her tongue, only then did I finally catch her eye, which I had been obstinately seeking, still not being able to cope with the fact that she had had time to forget what had occurred earlier in the morning – to forget it so thoroughly that upon meeting my glance, she replied with a blank questioning smile, and only after peering more closely did she remember suddenly what kind of answering smile I was expecting. Meanwhile, Ferdinand (the ladies having temporarily left the platform after pushing away their instruments like so many pieces of furniture) was juicily drawing his cronies' attention to the figure of an elderly luncher in a far corner of the café, who had, as some Frenchmen for some reason or other have, a little red ribbon or something on his coat lapel and whose gray beard combined with his mustaches to form a cozy yellowish nest for his sloppily munching mouth. Somehow the trappings of old age always amused Ferdie.

I did not stay long in Paris, but that week proved sufficient to engender between him and me that fake chumminess the imposing of which he had such a talent for. Subsequently I even turned out to be of some use to him: my firm acquired the film rights of one of his more intelligible stories, and then he had a good time pestering me with telegrams. As the years passed, we found ourselves every now and then beaming at each other in some place, but I never felt at ease in his presence, and that day in Fialta too I experienced a familiar depression upon learning that he was on the prowl nearby; one thing, however, considerably cheered me up: the flop of his recent play.

And here he was coming toward us, garbed in an absolutely waterproof coat with belt and pocket flaps, a camera across his shoulder, double rubber soles to his shoes, sucking with an imperturbability that was meant to be funny a long stick of moonstone candy, that specialty of Fialta's. Beside him walked the dapper, doll-like, rosy Segur, a lover of art and a perfect fool; I never could discover for what purpose Ferdinand needed him; and I still hear Nina exclaiming with a moaning tenderness that did not commit her to anything: 'Oh, he is such a darling, Segur!' They approached; Ferdinand and I greeted each other lustily, trying to crowd into handshake and backslap as much fervor as possible, knowing by experience that actually that was all but pretending it was only a preface; and it always happened like that: after every separation we met to the accompaniment of strings being excitedly tuned, in a bustle of geniality, in the hubbub of sentiments taking their seats; but the ushers would close the doors, and after that no one was admitted.

Segur complained to me about the weather, and at first I did not understand what he was talking about; even if the moist, gray, greenhouse essence of Fialta might be called 'weather,' it was just as much outside of anything that could serve us as a topic of conversation as was, for instance, Nina's slender elbow, which I was holding between finger and thumb, or a bit of tinfoil someone had dropped, shining in the middle of the cobbled street in the distance.

We four moved on, vague purchases still looming ahead. 'God, what an Indian!' Ferdinand suddenly exclaimed with fierce relish, violently nudging me and pointing at a poster. Farther on, near a fountain, he gave his stick of candy to a native child, a swarthy girl with beads round her pretty neck; we stopped to wait for him: he crouched saying something to her, addressing her sooty-black lowered eyelashes, and then he caught up with us, grinning and making one of those remarks with which he loved to spice his speech. Then his attention was drawn by an unfortunate object exhibited in a souvenir shop: a dreadful marble imitation of Mount St George showing a black tunnel at its base, which turned out to be the mouth of an inkwell, and with a compartment for pens in the semblance of railroad tracks. Open-mouthed, quivering, all agog with sardonic triumph, he turned that dusty, cumbersome, and perfectly irresponsible thing in his hands, paid without bargaining, and with his mouth still open came out carrying the monster. Like some autocrat who surrounds himself with hunchbacks and dwarfs, he would become attached to this or that hideous object; this infatuation might last from five minutes to several days or even longer if the thing happened to be animate.

Nina wistfully alluded to lunch, and seizing the opportunity when Ferdinand and Segur stopped at a post office, I hastened to lead her away. I still wonder what exactly she meant to me, that small dark woman of the narrow shoulders and 'lyrical limbs' (to quote the expression of a mincing émigré poet, one of the few men who had sighed platonically after her), and still less do I understand what was the purpose of fate in bringing us constantly together. I did not see her for quite a long while after my sojourn in Paris, and then one day when I came home from my office I found her having tea with my wife and examining on her silk-hosed hand, with her wedding ring gleaming through, the texture of some stockings bought cheap in Tauentzienstrasse. Once I was shown her photograph in a fashion magazine full of autumn leaves and gloves and windswept golf links. On a certain Christmas she sent me a picture postcard with snow and stars. On a Riviera beach she almost escaped my notice behind her dark glasses and terra-cotta tan. Another day, having dropped in on an ill-timed errand at the house of some strangers where a party was in progress, I saw her scarf and fur coat among alien scarecrows on a coatrack. In a bookshop she nodded to me from a page of one of her husband's stories, a page referring to an episodic servant girl, but smuggling in Nina in spite of the author's intention: 'Her face,' he wrote, 'was rather nature's snapshot than a meticulous portrait, so that when . . . tried to imagine it, all he could visualize were fleeting glimpses of disconnected features: the downy outline of her pommettes in the sun, the amber-tinted brown darkness of quick eyes, lips shaped into a friendly smile which was always ready to change into an ardent kiss.'

Again and again she hurriedly appeared in the margins of my life, without influencing in the least its basic text. One summer morning (Friday – because housemaids were thumping out carpets in the sun-dusted yard), my family was away in the country and I was lolling and smoking in bed when I heard the bell ring with tremendous violence – and there she was in the hall having burst in to leave (incidentally) a hairpin and (mainly) a trunk illuminated with hotel labels, which a fortnight later was retrieved for her by a nice Austrian boy, who (according to intangible but sure symptoms) belonged to the same very cosmopolitan association of which I was a member. Occasionally, in the middle of a conversation her name would be mentioned, and she would run down the steps of a chance sentence, without turning her head. While traveling in the Pyrenees, I spent a week at the château belonging to people with whom she and Ferdinand happened to be staying, and I shall never forget my first night there: how I waited, how certain I was that without my having to tell her she would steal to my room, how she did not come, and the din thousands of crickets made in the delirious depth of the rocky garden dripping with moonlight, the mad bubbling brooks, and my struggle between blissful southern fatigue after a long day of hunting on the screes and the wild thirst for her stealthy coming, low laugh, pink ankles above the swan's-down trimming of high-heeled slippers, but the night raved on, and she did not come, and when next day, in the course of a general ramble in the mountains, I told her of my waiting, she clasped her hands in dismay – and at once with a rapid glance estimated whether the backs of the gesticulating Ferd and his friend had sufficiently receded. I remember talking to her on the telephone across half of Europe (on her husband's business) and not recognizing at first her eager barking voice; and I remember once dreaming of her: I dreamt that my eldest girl had run in to tell me the doorman was sorely in trouble – and when I had gone down to him, I saw lying on a trunk, a roll of burlap under her head, pale-lipped and wrapped in a woolen kerchief, Nina fast asleep, as miserable refugees sleep in godforsaken railway stations. And regardless of what happened to me or to her, in between, we never discussed anything, as we never thought of each other during the intervals in our destiny, so that when we met the pace of life altered at once, all its atoms were recombined, and we lived in another, lighter time-medium, which was measured not by the lengthy separations but by those few meetings of which a short, supposedly frivolous life was thus artificially formed. And with each new meeting I grew more and more apprehensive; no – I did not experience any inner emotional collapse, the shadow of tragedy did not haunt our revels, my married life remained unimpaired, while on the other hand her eclectic husband ignored her casual affairs although deriving some profit from them in the way of pleasant and useful connections. I grew apprehensive because something lovely, delicate, and unrepeatable was being wasted: something which I abused by snapping off poor bright bits in gross haste while neglecting the modest but true core which perhaps it kept offering me in a pitiful whisper. I was apprehensive because, in the long run, I was somehow accepting Nina's life, the lies, the futility, the gibberish of that life. Even in the absence of any sentimental discord, I felt myself bound to seek, for a rational, if not moral, interpretation of my existence, and this meant choosing between the world in which I sat for my portrait, with my wife, my young daughters, the Doberman pinscher (idyllic garlands, a signet ring, a slender cane), between that happy, wise, and good world . . . and what? Was there any practical chance of life together with Nina, life I could barely imagine, for it would be penetrated, I knew, with a passionate, intolerable bitterness and every moment of it would be aware of a past, teeming with protean partners. No, the thing was absurd. And moreover was she not chained to her husband by something stronger than love – the staunch friendship between two convicts? Absurd! But then what should I have done with you, Nina, how should I have disposed of the store of sadness that had gradually accumulated as a result of our seemingly carefree, but really hopeless meetings?

Fialta consists of the old town and of the new one; here and there, past and present are interlaced, struggling either to disentangle themselves or to thrust each other out; each one has its own methods: the newcomer fights honestly – importing palm trees, setting up smart tourist agencies, painting with creamy lines the red smoothness of tennis courts; whereas the sneaky old-timer creeps out from behind a corner in the shape of some little street on crutches or the steps of stairs leading nowhere. On our way to the hotel, we passed a half-built white villa, full of litter within, on a wall of which again the same elephants, their monstrous baby knees wide apart, sat on huge, gaudy drums; in ethereal bundles the equestrienne (already with a penciled mustache) was resting on a broad-backed steed; and a tomato-nosed clown was walking a tightrope, balancing an umbrella ornamented with those recurrent stars – a vague symbolic recollection of the heavenly fatherland of circus performers. Here, in the Riviera part of Fialta, the wet gravel crunched in a more luxurious manner, and the lazy sighing of the sea was more audible. In the backyard of the hotel, a kitchen boy armed with a knife was pursuing a hen which was clucking madly as it raced for its life. A bootblack offered me his ancient throne with a toothless smile. Under the plane trees stood a motorcycle of German make, a mud-bespattered limousine, and a yellow long-bodied Icarus that looked like a giant scarab ('That's ours – Segur's, I mean,' said Nina, adding, 'Why don't you come with us, Victor?' although she knew very well that I could not come); in the lacquer of its elytra a gouache of sky and branches was engulfed; in the metal of one of the bomb-shaped lamps we ourselves were momentarily reflected, lean filmland pedestrians passing along the convex surface; and then, after a few steps, I glanced back and foresaw, in an almost optical sense, as it were, what really happened an hour or so later: the three of them wearing motoring helmets, getting in, smiling and waving to me, transparent to me like ghosts, with the color of the world shining through them, and then they were moving, receding, diminishing (Nina's last ten-fingered farewell); but actually the automobile was still standing quite motionless, smooth and whole like an egg, and Nina under my outstretched arm was entering a laurel-flanked doorway, and as we sat down we could see through the window Ferdinand and Segur, who had come by another way, slowly approaching.

There was no one on the veranda where we lunched except the Englishman I had recently observed; in front of him, a long glass containing a bright crimson drink threw an oval reflection on the tablecloth. In his eyes, I noticed the same bloodshot desire, but now it was in no sense related to Nina; that avid look was not directed at her at all, but was fixed on the upper right-hand corner of the broad window near which he was sitting.

Having pulled the gloves off her small thin hands, Nina, for the last time in her life, was eating the shellfish of which she was so fond. Ferdinand also busied himself with food, and I took advantage of his hunger to begin a conversation which gave me the semblance of power over him: to be specific, I mentioned his recent failure. After a brief period of fashionable religious conversion, during which grace descended upon him and he undertook some rather ambiguous pilgrimages, which ended in a decidedly scandalous adventure, he had turned his dull eyes toward barbarous Moscow. Now, frankly speaking, I have always been irritated by the complacent conviction that a ripple of stream of consciousness, a few healthy obscenities, and a dash of communism in any old slop pail will alchemically and automatically produce ultramodern literature; and I will contend until I am shot that art as soon as it is brought into contact with politics inevitably sinks to the level of any ideological trash. In Ferdinand's case, it is true, all this was rather irrelevant: the muscles of his muse were exceptionally strong, to say nothing of the fact that he didn't care a damn for the plight of the underdog; but because of certain obscurely mischievous undercurrents of that sort, his art had become still more repulsive. Except for a few snobs none had understood the play; I had not seen it myself, but could well imagine that elaborate Kremlinesque night along the impossible spirals of which he spun various wheels of dismembered symbols; and now, not without pleasure, I asked him whether he had read a recent bit of criticism about himself.

'Criticism!' he exclaimed. 'Fine criticism! Every slick jackanapes sees fit to read me a lecture. Ignorance of my work is their bliss. My books are touched gingerly, as one touches something that may go bang. Criticism! They are examined from every point of view except the essential one. It is as if a naturalist, in describing the equine genus, started to jaw about saddles or Mme de V.' (he named a well-known literary hostess who indeed strongly resembled a grinning horse). 'I would like some of that pigeon's blood too,' he continued in the same loud, ripping voice, addressing the waiter, who understood his desire only after he had looked in the direction of the long-nailed finger which unceremoniously pointed at the Englishman's glass. For some reason or other, Segur mentioned Ruby Rose, the lady who painted flowers on her breast, and the conversation took on a less insulting character. Meanwhile the big Englishman suddenly made up his mind, got up on a chair, stepped from there on to the windowsill, and stretched up till he reached that coveted corner of the frame where rested a compact furry moth, which he deftly slipped into a pillbox.

'. . . rather like Wouwerman's white horse,' said Ferdinand, in regard to something he was discussing with Segur.

'*Tu es très hippique ce matin*,' remarked the latter.

Soon they both left to telephone. Ferdinand was particularly fond of long-distance calls, and particularly good at endowing them, no matter what the distance, with a friendly warmth when it was necessary, as for instance now, to make sure of free lodgings.

From afar came the sounds of music – a trumpet, a zither. Nina and I set out to wander again. The circus on its way to Fialta had apparently sent out runners: an advertising pageant was tramping by; but we did not catch its head, as it had turned uphill into a side alley: the gilded back of some carriage was receding, a man in a burnoose led a camel, a file of four mediocre Indians carried placards on poles, and behind them, by special permission, a tourist's small son in a sailor suit sat reverently on a tiny pony.

We wandered by a café where the tables were now almost dry but still empty; the waiter was examining (I hope he adopted it later) a horrible foundling, the absurd inkstand affair, stowed by Ferdinand on the banisters in passing. At the next corner we were attracted by an old stone stairway, and we climbed up, and I kept looking at the sharp angle of Nina's step as she ascended, raising her skirt, its narrowness requiring the same gesture as formerly length had done; she diffused a familiar warmth, and going up beside her, I recalled the last time we had come together. It had been in a Paris house, with many people around, and my dear friend Jules Darboux, wishing to do me a refined aesthetic favor, had touched my sleeve and said, 'I want you to meet –' and led me to Nina, who sat in the corner of a couch, her body folded Z-wise, with an ashtray at her heel, and she took a long turquoise cigarette holder from her lips and joyfully, slowly exclaimed, 'Well, of all people –' and then all evening my heart felt like breaking, as I passed from group to group with a sticky glass in my fist, now and then looking at her from a distance (she did not look . . .), and listened to scraps of conversation, and overheard one man saying to another, 'Funny, how they all smell alike, burnt leaf through whatever perfume they use, those angular dark-haired girls,' and as it often happens, a trivial remark related to some unknown topic coiled and clung to one's own intimate recollection, a parasite of its sadness.

At the top of the steps, we found ourselves on a rough kind of terrace. From here one could see the delicate outline of the dove-colored Mount St George with a cluster of bone-white flecks (some hamlet) on one of its slopes; the smoke of an indiscernible train undulated along its rounded base – and suddenly disappeared; still lower, above the jumble of roofs, one could perceive a solitary cypress, resembling the moist-twirled black tip of a watercolor brush; to the right, one caught a glimpse of the sea, which was gray, with silver wrinkles. At our feet lay a rusty old key, and on the wall of the half-ruined house adjoining the terrace, the ends of some wire still remained hanging . . . I reflected that formerly there had been life here, a family had enjoyed the coolness at nightfall, clumsy children had colored pictures by the light of a lamp . . . We lingered there as if listening to something; Nina, who stood on higher ground, put a hand on my shoulder and smiled, and carefully, so as not to crumple her smile, kissed me. With an unbearable force, I relived (or so it now seems to me) all that had ever been between us beginning with a similar kiss; and I said (substituting for our cheap, formal 'thou' that strangely full and expressive 'you' to which the circumnavigator, enriched all around, returns), 'Look here – what if I love you?' Nina glanced at me, I repeated those words, I wanted to add . . . but something like a bat passed swiftly across her face, a quick, queer, almost ugly expression, and she, who would utter coarse words with perfect simplicity, became embarrassed; I also felt awkward . . . 'Never mind, I was only joking,' I hastened to say, lightly encircling her waist. From somewhere a firm bouquet of small, dark, unselfishly smelling violets appeared in her hands, and before she returned to her husband and car, we stood for a little while longer by the stone parapet, and our romance was even more hopeless than it had ever been. But the stone was as warm as flesh, and suddenly I understood something I had been seeing without understanding – why a piece of tinfoil had sparkled so on the pavement, why the gleam of a glass had trembled on a tablecloth, why the sea was ashimmer: somehow, by imperceptible degrees, the white sky above Fialta had got saturated with sunshine, and now it was sun-pervaded throughout, and this brimming white radiance grew broader and broader, all dissolved in it, all vanished, all passed, and I stood on the station platform of Mlech with a freshly bought newspaper, which told me that the yellow car I had seen under the plane trees had suffered a crash beyond Fialta, having run at full speed into the truck of a traveling circus entering the town, a crash from which Ferdinand and his friend, those invulnerable rogues, those salamanders of fate, those basilisks of good fortune, had escaped with local and temporary injury to their scales, while Nina, in spite of her long-standing, faithful imitation of them, had turned out after all to be mortal.

The Doorbell

Seven years had passed since he and she had parted in Petersburg. God, what a crush there had been at the Nikolaevsky Station! Don't stand so close – the train is about to start. Well, here we go, good-bye, dearest . . . She walked alongside, tall, thin, wearing a raincoat, with a black-and-white scarf around her neck, and a slow current carried her off backward. A Red Army recruit, he took part, reluctantly and confusedly, in the civil war. Then, one beautiful night, to the ecstatic stridulation of prairie crickets, he went over to the Whites. A year later, in 1920, not long before leaving Russia, on the steep, stony Chainaya Street in Yalta, he ran into his uncle, a Moscow lawyer. Why, yes, there was news – two letters. She was leaving for Germany and already had obtained a passport. You look fine, young man. And at last Russia let go of him – a permanent leave, according to some. Russia had held him for a long time; he had slowly slithered down from north to south, and Russia kept trying to keep him in her grasp, with the taking of Tver, Kharkov, Belgorod, and various interesting little villages, but it was no use. She had in store for him one last temptation, one last gift – the Crimea – but even that did not help. He left. And on board the ship he made the acquaintance of a young Englishman, a jolly chap and an athlete, who was on his way to Africa.

Nikolay visited Africa, and Italy, and for some reason the Canary Islands, and then Africa again, where he served for a while in the Foreign Legion. At first he recalled her often, then rarely, then again more and more often. Her second husband, the German industrialist Kind, died during the war. He had owned a goodish bit of real estate in Berlin, and Nikolay assumed there was no danger of her going hungry there. But how quickly time passed! Amazing! . . . Had seven whole years really gone by?

During those years he had grown hardier, rougher, had lost an index finger, and had learned two languages – Italian and English. The color of his eyes had become lighter and their expression more candid owing to the smooth rustic tan that covered his face. He smoked a pipe. His walk, which had always had the solidity characteristic of short-legged people, now acquired a remarkable rhythm. One thing about him had not changed at all: his laugh, accompanied by a quip and a twinkle.

He had quite a time, chuckling softly and shaking his head, before he finally decided to drop everything and by easy stages make his way to Berlin. On one occasion – at a newsstand, somewhere in Italy, he noticed an émigré Russian paper, published in Berlin. He wrote to the paper to place an advertisement under Personal: So-and-so seeks So-and-so. He got no reply. On a side trip to Corsica, he met a fellow Russian, the old journalist Grushevski, who was leaving for Berlin. Make inquiries on my behalf. Perhaps you'll find her. Tell her I am alive and well . . . But this source did not bring any news either. Now it was high time to take Berlin by storm. There, on the spot, the search would be simpler. He had a lot of trouble obtaining a German visa, and he was running out of funds. Oh, well, he would get there one way or another . . .

And so he did. Wearing a trenchcoat and a checked cap, short and broad-shouldered, with a pipe between his teeth and a battered valise in his good hand, he exited on to the square in front of the station. There he stopped to admire a great jewel-bright advertisement that inched its way through the darkness, then vanished and started again from another point. He spent a bad night in a stuffy room in a cheap hotel, trying to think of ways to begin the search. The address bureau, the office of the Russian-language newspaper . . . Seven years. She must really have aged. It was rotten of him to have waited so long; he could have come sooner. But, ah, those years, that stupendous roaming about the world, the obscure ill-paid jobs, chances taken and chucked, the excitement of freedom, the freedom he had dreamed of in childhood! . . . It was pure Jack London . . . And here he was again: a new city, a suspiciously itchy featherbed, and the screech of a late tram. He groped for his matches, and with a habitual movement of his index stump began pressing the soft tobacco into the pipe-bowl.

When traveling the way he did you forget the names of time; they are crowded out by those of places. In the morning, when Nikolay went out intending to go to the police station, the gratings were down on all the shop fronts. It was a damned Sunday. So much for the address office and the newspaper. It was also late autumn: windy weather, asters in the public gardens, a sky of solid white, yellow trees, yellow trams, the nasal honking of rheumy taxis. A chill of excitement came over him at the idea that he was in the same town as she. A fifty-pfennig coin bought him a glass of port in a cab drivers' bar, and the wine on an empty stomach had a pleasant effect. Here and there in the streets there came a sprinkling of Russian speech: '. . . *Skol'ko raz ya tebe govorila*' ('. . . How many times have I told you').

And again, after the passage of several natives: '. . . He's willing to sell them to me, but frankly, I . . .' The excitement made him chuckle and finish each pipeful much more quickly than usual. '. . . Seemed to be gone, but now Grisha's down with it too . . .' He considered going up to the next pair of Russians and asking, very politely: 'Do you know by any chance Olga Kind, born Countess Karski?' They must all know each other in this bit of provincial Russia gone astray.

It was already evening, and, in the twilight, a beautiful tangerine light had filled the glassed tiers of a huge department store when Nikolay noticed, on one of the sides of a front door, a small white sign that said: 'I. S. WEINER, DENTIST, FROM PETROGRAD.' An unexpected recollection virtually scalded him. This fine friend of ours is pretty well decayed and must go. In the window, right in front of the torture seat, inset glass photographs displayed Swiss landscapes . . . The window gave on Moika Street. Rinse, please. And Dr Weiner, a fat, placid, white-gowned old man in perspicacious glasses, sorted his tinkling instruments. She used to go to him for treatment, and so did his cousins, and they even used to say to each other, when they quarreled for some reason or other, 'How would you like a Weiner?' (i.e., a punch in the mouth). Nikolay dallied in front of the door, on the point of ringing the bell, remembering it was Sunday; he thought some more and rang anyway. There was a buzzing in the lock and the door gave. He went up one flight. A maid opened the door. 'No, the doctor is not receiving today.' 'My teeth are fine,' objected Nikolay in very poor German. 'Dr Weiner is an old friend of mine. My name is Galatov – I'm sure he remembers me . . .' 'I'll tell him,' said the maid.

A moment later a middle-aged man in a frogged velveteen jacket came out into the hallway. He had a carroty complexion and seemed extremely friendly. After a cheerful greeting he added in Russian, 'I don't remember you, though – there must be a mistake.' Nikolay looked at him and apologized: 'Afraid so. I don't remember you either. I was expecting to find the Dr Weiner who lived on Moika Street in Petersburg before the Revolution, but got the wrong one. Sorry.'

'Oh, that must be a namesake of mine. A common namesake. I lived on Zagorodny Avenue.'

'We all used to go to him,' explained Nikolay, 'and well, I thought . . . You see, I'm trying to locate a certain lady, a Madame Kind, that's the name of her second husband –'

Weiner bit his lip, looked away with an intent expression, then addressed him again. 'Wait a minute . . . I seem to recall . . . I seem to recall a Madame Kind who came to see me here not long ago and was also under the impression – We'll know for sure in a minute. Be kind enough to step into my office.'

The office remained a blur in Nikolay's vision. He did not take his eyes off Weiner's impeccable calvities as the latter bent over his appointment book.

'We'll know for sure in a minute,' he repeated, sunning his fingers across the pages. 'We'll know for sure in just a minute. We'll know in just . . . Here we are. Frau Kind. Gold filling and some other work – which I can't make out, there's a blot here.'

'And what's the first name and patronymic?' asked Nikolay, approaching the table and almost knocking off an ashtray with his cuff.

'That's in the book too. Olga Kirillovna.'

'Right,' said Nikolay with a sigh of relief.

'The address is Plannerstrasse fifty-nine, care of Babb,' said Weiner with a smack of his lips, and rapidly copied the address on a separate slip. 'Second street from here. Here you are. Very happy to be of service. Is she a relative of yours?'

'My mother,' replied Nikolay.

Coming out of the dentist's, he proceeded with a somewhat quickened step. Finding her so easily astonished him, like a card trick. He had never paused to think, while traveling to Berlin, that she might long since have died or moved to a different city, and yet the trick had worked. Weiner had turned out to be a different Weiner – and yet fate found a way. Beautiful city, beautiful rain! (The pearly autumn drizzle seemed to fall in a whisper and the streets were dark.) How would she greet him – tenderly? Sadly? Or with complete calm. She had not spoiled him as a child. You are forbidden to run through the drawing room while I am playing the piano. As he grew up, he would feel more and more frequently that she did not have much use for him. Now he tried to picture her face, but his thoughts obstinately refused to take on color, and he simply could not gather in a living optical image what he knew in his mind: her tall, thin figure with that loosely assembled look about her; her dark hair with streaks of gray at the temples; her large, pale mouth; the old raincoat she had on the last time he saw her; and the tired, bitter expression of an aging woman, that seemed to have always been on her face – even before the death of his father, Admiral Galatov, who had shot himself shortly before the Revolution. Number 51. Eight houses more.

He suddenly realized that he was unendurably, indecently perturbed, much more so than he had been, for example, that first time when he lay pressing his sweat-drenched body against the side of a cliff and aiming at an approaching whirlwind, a white scarecrow on a splendid Arabian horse. He stopped just short of Number 59, took out his pipe and a rubber tobacco pouch; stuffed the bowl slowly and carefully, without spilling a single shred; lit up, coddled the flame, drew, watched the fiery mound swell, gulped a mouthful of sweetish, tongue-prickling smoke, carefully expelled it, and with a firm, unhurried step walked up to the house.

The stairs were so dark that he stumbled a couple of times. When, in the dense blackness, he reached the second-floor landing, he struck a match and made out a gilt nameplate. Wrong name. It was only much higher that he found the odd name 'Babb.' The flamelet burned his fingers and went out. God, my heart is pounding . . . He groped for the bell in the dark and rang. Then he removed the pipe from between his teeth and began waiting, feeling an agonizing smile rend his mouth.

Then he heard a lock, a bolt made a double resonant sound, and the door, as if swung by a violent wind, burst open. It was just as dark in the anteroom as on the stairs, and out of that darkness floated a vibrant, joyful voice. 'The lights are out in the whole building – *eto oozhas*, it's appalling' – and Nikolay recognized at once that long emphatic 'oo' and on its basis instantly reconstructed down to the most minute feature the person who now stood, still concealed by darkness, in the doorway.

'Sure, can't see a thing,' said he with a laugh, and advanced toward her.

Her cry was as startled as if a strong hand had struck her. In the dark he found her arms, and shoulders, and bumped against something (probably the umbrella stand). 'No, no, it's not possible . . .' she kept repeating rapidly as she backed away.

'Hold still, Mother, hold still for a minute,' he said, hitting something again (this time it was the half-open front door, which shut with a great slam).

'It can't be . . . Nicky, Nick –'

He was kissing her at random, on the cheeks, on the hair, everywhere, unable to see anything in the dark but with some interior vision recognizing all of her from head to toe, and only one thing about her had changed (and even this novelty unexpectedly made him recall his earliest childhood, when she used to play the piano): the strong, elegant smell of perfume – as if those intervening years had not existed, the years of his adolescence and her widowhood, when she no longer wore perfume and faded so sorrowfully – it seemed as if nothing of that had happened, and he had passed straight from distant exile into childhood . . . 'It's you. You've come. You're really here,' she prattled, pressing her soft lips against him. 'It's good . . . This is how it should be . . .'

'Isn't there any light anywhere?' Nikolay inquired cheerfully.

She opened an inner door and said excitedly, 'Yes, come on. I've lit some candles there.'

'Well, let me look at you,' he said, entering the flickering aura of candlelight and gazing avidly at his mother. Her dark hair had been bleached a very light strawlike shade.

'Well, don't you recognize me?' she asked, with a nervous intake of breath, then added hurriedly, 'Don't stare at me like that. Come on, tell me all the news! What a tan you have . . . my goodness! Yes, tell me everything!'

That blonde bob . . . And her face was made up with excruciating care. The moist streak of a tear, though, had eaten through the rosy paint, and her mascara-laden lashes were wet, and the powder on the wings of her nose had turned violet. She was wearing a glossy blue dress closed at the throat. And everything about her was unfamiliar, restless and frightening.

'You're probably expecting company, Mother,' observed Nikolay, and not quite knowing what to say next, energetically threw off his overcoat.

She moved away from him toward the table, which was set for a meal and sparkled with crystal in the semi-darkness; then she came back toward him, and mechanically glanced at herself in the shadow-blurred mirror.

'So many years have passed . . . Goodness! I can hardly

believe my eyes. Oh, yes, I have friends coming tonight. I'll call them off. I'll phone them. I'll do something. I must call them off . . . Oh, Lord . . .'

She pressed against him, palpating him to find out how real he was.

'Calm down, Mother, what's the matter with you – this is overdoing it. Let's sit down somewhere. *Comment vas-tu?* How does life treat you?' . . . And, for some reason fearing the answers to his questions, he started telling her about himself, in the snappy neat way he had, puffing on his pipe, trying to drown his astonishment in words and smoke. It turned out that, after all, she had seen his ad and had been in touch with the old journalist and been on the point of writing to Nikolay – always on the point . . . Now that he had seen her face distorted by its make-up and her artificially fair hair he felt that her voice, too, was no longer the same. And as he described his adventures, without a moment's pause, he glanced around the half-lit, quivering room, at its awful middle-class trappings – the toy cat on the mantelpiece, the coy screen from behind which protruded the foot of the bed, the picture of Friedrich the Great playing the flute, the bookless shelf with the little vases in which the reflected lights darted up and down like mercury . . . As his eyes roamed around he also inspected something he had previously only noticed in passing:

that table – a table set for two, with liqueurs, a bottle of Asti, two tall wine glasses, and an enormous pink cake adorned with a ring of still unlit little candles. '. . . Of course, I immediately jumped out of my tent, and what do you think it turned out to be? Come on, guess!'

She seemed to emerge from a trance, and gave him a wild look (she was reclining next to him on the divan, her temples compressed between her hands, and her peach-colored stockings gave off an unfamiliar sheen).

'Aren't you listening, Mother?'

'Why, yes – I am . . .'

And now he noticed something else: she was oddly absent, as if she were listening not to his words but to a doomful thing coming from afar, menacing and inevitable. He went on with his jolly narrative, but then stopped again and asked, 'That cake – in whose honor is it? Looks awfully good.'

His mother responded with a flustered smile. 'Oh, it's a little stunt. I told you I was expecting company.'

'It reminded me awfully of Petersburg,' said Nikolay. 'Remember how you once made a mistake and forgot one candle? I had turned ten, but there were only nine candles. *Tu escamotas* my birthday. I bawled my head off. And how many do we have here?'

'Oh, what does it matter?' she shouted, and rose, almost as if she wanted to block his view of the table.

'Why don't you tell me instead what time it is? I must ring up and cancel the party . . . I must do something.'

'Quarter past seven,' said Nikolay.

'*Trop tard, trop tard!*' she raised her voice again. 'All right! At this point it no longer matters . . .'

Both fell silent. She resumed her seat. Nikolay was trying to force himself to hug her, to cuddle up to her, to ask, 'Listen, Mother – what has happened to you? Come on: out with it.' He took another look at the brilliant table and counted the candles ringing the cake. There were twenty-five of them. Twenty-five! And he was already twenty-eight . . .

'Please don't examine my room like that!' said his mother. 'You look like a regular detective! It's a horrid hole. I would gladly move elsewhere, but I sold the villa that Kind left me.' Abruptly she gave a small gasp: 'Wait a minute – what was that? Did you make that noise?'

'Yes,' answered Nikolay. 'I'm knocking the ashes out of my pipe. But tell me: you do still have enough money? You're not having any trouble making ends meet?'

She busied herself with readjusting a ribbon on her sleeve and spoke without looking at him: 'Yes . . . Of course. He left me a few foreign stocks, a hospital and an ancient prison. A prison! . . . But I must warn you that I have barely enough to live on. For heaven's sake stop knocking with that pipe. I must warn you that I . . .

That I cannot . . . Oh, you understand, Nick – it would be hard for me to support you.'

'What on earth are you talking about, Mother?' exclaimed Nikolay (and at that moment, like a stupid sun issuing from behind a stupid cloud, the electric light burst forth from the ceiling). 'There, we can snuff out those tapers now; it was like squatting in the Mostaga Mausoleum. You see, I do have a small supply of cash, and anyway, I like to be as free as a damned fowl of some sort . . . Come, sit down – stop running around the room.'

Tall, thin, bright blue, she stopped in front of him and now, in the full light, he saw how much she had aged, how insistently the wrinkles on her cheeks and forehead showed through the make-up. And that awful bleached hair! . . .

'You came tumbling in so suddenly,' she said and, biting her lips, she consulted a small clock standing on the shelf. 'Like snow out of a cloudless sky . . . It's fast. No, it's stopped. I'm having company tonight, and here you arrive. It's a crazy situation . . .'

'Nonsense, Mother. They'll come, they'll see your son has arrived, and very soon they'll evaporate. And before the evening's over you and I will go to some music hall, and have supper somewhere . . . I remember seeing an African show – that was really something!

Imagine – about fifty Negroes, and a rather large, the size of, say –'

The doorbell buzzed loudly in the front hall. Olga Kirillovna, who had perched on the arm of a chair, gave a start and straightened up.

Wait, I'll get it,' said Nikolay, rising.

She caught him by the sleeve. Her face was twitching. The bell stopped. The caller waited.

It must be your guests,' said Nikolay. 'Your twenty-five guests. We have to let them in.'

His mother gave a brusque shake of her head and resumed listening intently.

It isn't right –' began Nikolay.

She pulled at his sleeve, whispering, 'Don't you dare! I don't want to . . . Don't you dare . . .'

The bell started buzzing again, insistently and irritably this time. And it buzzed on for a long time.

'Let me go,' said Nikolay. 'This is silly. If somebody rings you have to answer the door. What are you frightened of?'

'Don't you dare – do you hear,' she repeated, spasmodically clutching at his hand. 'I implore you . . . Nicky, Nicky, Nicky! . . . Don't!'

The bell stopped. It was replaced by a series of vigorous knocks, produced, it seemed, by the stout knob of a cane.

Nikolay headed resolutely for the front hall. But before he reached it his mother had grabbed him by the shoulders, and tried with all her might to drag him back, whispering all the while, 'Don't you dare . . . Don't you dare . . . For God's sake! . . .'

The bell sounded again, briefly and angrily.

'It's your business,' said Nikolay with a laugh and, thrusting his hands into his pockets, walked the length of the room. This is a real nightmare, he thought, and chuckled again.

The ringing had stopped. All was still. Apparently the ringer had got fed up and left. Nikolay went up to the table, contemplated the splendid cake with its bright frosting and twenty-five festive candles, and the two wineglasses. Nearby, as if hiding in the bottle's shadow, lay a small white cardboard box. He picked it up and took off the lid. It contained a brand-new, rather tasteless silver cigarette case.

'And that's that,' said Nikolay.

His mother, who was half-reclining on the couch with her face buried in a cushion, was convulsed with sobs. In previous years he had often seen her cry, but then she had cried quite differently: while sitting at table, for instance, she would cry without turning her face away, and blow her nose loudly, and talk, talk, talk; yet now she was weeping so girlishly, was lying there with such abandon . . . and there was something so graceful about the curve of her spine and about the way one foot, in its velvet slipper, was touching the floor . . . One might almost think that it was a young, blonde woman crying. . . . And her crumpled handkerchief was lying on the carpet just the way it was supposed to, in that pretty scene.

Nikolay uttered a Russian grunt (*kryak*) and sat down on the edge of her couch. He *kryak*'ed again. His mother, still hiding her face, said into the cushion, 'Oh, why couldn't you have come earlier? Even one year earlier . . . Just one year! . . .'

'I wouldn't know,' said Nikolay.

'It's all over now,' she sobbed, and tossed her light hair. 'All over. I'll be fifty in May. Grown-up son comes to see aged mother. And why did you have to come right at this moment . . . tonight!'

Nikolay put on his overcoat (which, contrary to European custom he had simply thrown into a corner), took his cap out of a pocket, and sat down by her again.

'Tomorrow morning I'll move on,' he said, stroking the shiny blue silk of his mother's shoulder. 'I feel an urge to head north now, to Norway, perhaps – or else out to sea for some whale fishing. I'll write you. In a year or so we'll meet again, then perhaps I'll stay longer. Don't be cross with me because of my wanderlust!'

Quickly she embraced him and pressed a wet cheek to his neck. Then she squeezed his hand and suddenly cried out in astonishment.

'Blown off by a bullet,' laughed Nikolay. 'Good-bye, my dearest.'

She felt the smooth stub of his finger and gave it a cautious kiss. Then she put her arm around her son and walked with him to the door.

'Please write often . . . Why are you laughing? All the powder must have come off my face?'

And no sooner had the door shut after him than she flew, her blue dress rustling, to the telephone.

Ryūnosuke Akutagawa *Hell Screen*
Kingsley Amis *Dear Illusion*
Donald Barthelme *Some of Us Had Been Threatening Our Friend Colby*
Samuel Beckett *The Expelled*
Saul Bellow *Him With His Foot in His Mouth*
Jorge Luis Borges *The Widow Ching – Pirate*
Paul Bowles *The Delicate Prey*
Italo Calvino *The Queen's Necklace*
Albert Camus *The Adulterous Woman*
Truman Capote *Children on Their Birthdays*
Angela Carter *Bluebeard*
Raymond Chandler *Killer in the Rain*
Eileen Chang *Red Rose, White Rose*
G. K. Chesterton *The Strange Crime of John Boulnois*
Joseph Conrad *Youth*
Robert Coover *Romance of the Thin Man and the Fat Lady*
Isak Dinesen [Karen Blixen] *Babette's Feast*
Margaret Drabble *The Gifts of War*
Hans Fallada *Short Treatise on the Joys of Morphinism*
F. Scott Fitzgerald *Babylon Revisited*
Ian Fleming *The Living Daylights*
E. M. Forster *The Machine Stops*
Shirley Jackson *The Tooth*
Henry James *The Beast in the Jungle*

M. R. James *Canon Alberic's Scrap-Book*
James Joyce *Two Gallants*
Franz Kafka *In the Penal Colony*
Rudyard Kipling *'They'*
D. H. Lawrence *Odour of Chrysanthemums*
Primo Levi *The Magic Paint*
H. P. Lovecraft *The Colour Out of Space*
Malcolm Lowry *Lunar Caustic*
Carson McCullers *Wunderkind*
Katherine Mansfield *Bliss*
Robert Musil *Flypaper*
Vladimir Nabokov *Terra Incognita*
R. K. Narayan *A Breath of Lucifer*
Frank O'Connor *The Cornet-Player Who Betrayed Ireland*
Dorothy Parker *The Sexes*
Ludmilla Petrushevskaya *Through the Wall*
Jean Rhys *La Grosse Fifi*
Saki *Filboid Studge, the Story of a Mouse That Helped*
Isaac Bashevis Singer *The Last Demon*
William Trevor *The Mark-2 Wife*
John Updike *Rich in Russia*
H. G. Wells *The Door in the Wall*
Eudora Welty *Moon Lake*
P. G. Wodehouse *The Crime Wave at Blandings*
Virginia Woolf *The Lady in the Looking-Glass*
Stefan Zweig *Chess*

a little history

Penguin Modern Classics were launched in 1961, and have been shaping the reading habits of generations ever since.

The list began with distinctive grey spines and evocative pictorial covers – a look that, after various incarnations, continues to influence their current design – and with books that are still considered landmark classics today.

Penguin Modern Classics have caused scandal and political change, inspired great films and broken down barriers, whether social, sexual or the boundaries of language itself. They remain the most provocative, groundbreaking, exciting and revolutionary works of the last 100 years (or so).

In 2011, on the fiftieth anniversary of the Modern Classics, we're publishing fifty Mini Modern Classics: the very best short fiction by writers ranging from Beckett to Conrad, Nabokov to Saki, Updike to Wodehouse. Though they don't take long to read, they'll stay with you long after you turn the final page.